Class No. _____J9-11_____ Acc No. _C/228202_

Author: _Cliff, A_ Loc: _____

LEABHARLANN
CHONDAE AN CHABHAIN

_____

_____

_____

1. **This book may be kept three weeks. It is to be returned on / before the last date stamped below.**
2. **A fine of 25c will be charged for every week or part of week a book is overdue.** (Code 23)

Books by Alex Cliff
SUPERPOWERS series

SUPER

THE CLASH OF CLAWS

POWERS

ALEX CLIFF

ILLUSTRATED BY LEO HARTAS

PUFFIN

PUFFIN BOOKS

Published by the Penguin Group
Penguin Books Ltd, 80 Strand, London WC2R ORL, England
Penguin Group (USA) Inc., 375 Hudson Street, New York, New York 10014, USA
Penguin Group (Canada), 90 Eglinton Avenue East, Suite 700, Toronto, Ontario, Canada M4P 2Y3
(a division of Pearson Penguin Canada Inc.)
Penguin Ireland, 25 St Stephen's Green, Dublin 2, Ireland (a division of Penguin Books Ltd)
Penguin Group (Australia), 250 Camberwell Road, Camberwell, Victoria 3124, Australia
(a division of Pearson Australia Group Pty Ltd)
Penguin Books India Pvt Ltd, 11 Community Centre, Panchsheel Park,
New Delhi – 110 017, India
Penguin Group (NZ), 67 Apollo Drive, Rosedale, North Shore 0632, New Zealand
(a division of Pearson New Zealand Ltd)
Penguin Books (South Africa) (Pty) Ltd, 24 Sturdee Avenue, Rosebank,
Johannesburg 2196, South Africa

Penguin Books Ltd, Registered Offices: 80 Strand, London WC2R ORL, England

puffinbooks.com

Published 2007
1

The moral right of the author and illustrator has been asserted

Set in Bembo
Typeset by Palimpsest Book Production Limited, Grangemouth, Stirlingshire
Made and printed in England by Clays Ltd, St Ives plc

British Library Cataloguing in Publication Data
A CIP catalogue record for this book is available from the British Library

ISBN: 978-0-141-32137-0

To Steve Cole, for being a genius writer (ha!),
inspiration, source of silly jokes and best friend.
These books couldn't have been
written without you.
PS You're not always right, though,
I still think geese are scary and pigs
can snort threateningly!

CONTENTS

JUST IMAGINE . . .

a full moon shining down on a ruined
castle. In the nearby village the church
bells strike midnight. A hawk flies
through the darkness into the castle.
There is a loud crash of thunder. As the
echo of the thunder fades, the evil
goddess Juno appears in the doorway of
the castle's only remaining tower. She is
twice as tall as a normal woman. A

cloak of feathers swirls from her shoulders and her black eyes flash in anger.

'Worms!' she hisses, snapping her fingers. 'Maggots!'

With a creaking, grinding noise some of the stones on the inside of the tower wall opposite her begin to crumble away.

A man looks out of the hole in the wall. His face is lined with deep wrinkles. It is the superhero Hercules. 'I imagine you must be talking about the boys, Finlay and Max?' he asks. There is a note of amusement in his deep voice as he looks at the enraged goddess.

'Pathetic humans!' Juno spits out.

'Pathetic?' Hercules raises his eyebrows. 'I hardly see how you can call

those two boys that, Juno. You have set
them four tasks and they have
completed each one, winning back four
of my superpowers for me.'

'I still hold your three remaining
superpowers,' Juno reminds him. 'You
will not get *them* back!'

'I believe I will, Juno.' Hercules meets the goddess's gaze squarely. 'The deal you made with them still stands. There are only three remaining tasks of the seven you set them and every time that they succeed in completing another task, they win back another of my superpowers. I believe that soon all my powers will be returned to me and I shall break free from this prison.' He thumps the wall of the tower.

'Never!' Juno shrieks in rage. 'In the morning, the boys must slay the Man-Eating Birds of Stymphalia. Are you really trying to tell me that they will be able to do that?'

'Yes,' Hercules declares. 'I am!'

The goddess and the superhero stare
at each other.

When Juno speaks her voice is low
and dangerous. 'They will fail.' Before
Hercules can speak she clicks her
fingers. The stones instantly re-form,

shutting Hercules in his dark prison again.

Juno looks at the wall where the hole has been. Her eyes glitter dangerously. 'And this time they die, Hercules.'

She claps her hands. There is a crash of thunder and the next second, a hawk can be seen swooping out of the tower and flying away into the dark night.

CHAPTER ONE

A GREAT DAY OUT

Max Hayward stared at his mum over the breakfast table. Had he really just heard right? 'What?' he exclaimed. 'We're going out for the day? But we can't be, Mum!'

'Why not?' Mrs Hayward said in surprise. 'It'll be fun. We're going to Haslemere House.' She cleared away the cereal bowls. 'I rang Finlay's mum after you went to bed last night and he's coming too. You'll both have a great time. The website said there are ancient suits of armour inside the house as well as big gardens and a maze.'

'But we were going to go to the castle, Mum,' Max protested.

'Oh, Max, you've been at the castle every day this half-term,' Mrs Hayward said. 'Isn't it getting a bit boring?'

Pictures of the last few days flashed into Max's mind – finding Hercules trapped in a tower there, meeting the goddess Juno, striking a deal with her to get Hercules' superpowers back, fighting a sabre-toothed lion, killing the Nine-Headed River Monster, cleaning a thousand years of

poo out of a stables and chasing a giant
wild boar . . .

No, he could *definitely* say it hadn't
been boring! 'No, Mum, it's . . . it's fun
there,' he said. *If you like getting bitten,
chased and attacked*, he thought to
himself.

'Well, I'm sorry, Max, but the plans are all made,' his mum said firmly. 'Auntie Carol's coming too, with your cousin, Zoë, and Zoë's best friend, Michelle.' The phone started ringing and she broke off to answer it. 'Hello?' She listened for a moment. 'It's Fin, for you,' she said, handing Max the phone.

Max took the phone through to the lounge. 'Hi.'

'Max! What's going on?' Finlay shouted down the phone, almost shattering Max's eardrum. 'I woke up this morning and my mum said I'm coming out for the day with you! What about the task? What about Hercules? We *can't* go out for the day!'

'I know!' Max replied desperately. 'But Mum says I've got to. Look, maybe you can get out of it and get started on the task, then I can meet you at the castle later?'

He held his breath. He couldn't bear the thought of having to go round some boring house while Finlay was up at the castle using one of Hercules' superpowers and risking his life fighting a flock of man-eating birds, but at least that way there was a chance that they might get the next task done before sunset.

'No,' Finlay said firmly. 'We're in this together.'

Max felt a rush of relief.

'Anyway,' Finlay went on, and Max could hear the grin in his voice. 'You don't think I'm going to fight a load of man-eating birds on my own, do you? No way!'

'What are we going to do, then?' Max demanded. He saw a bouncy ball on the table and picked it up, bouncing it against the tabletop as he tried to think of a way out.

'I know,' Finlay said. 'Why don't we go to this Haslemere House place and then when we get there, we say we feel sick, so your mum has to bring us home. By the time we're back here we can say we're OK again and then go up to the castle and do the task.'

'But what about getting the superpower?' Max asked.

The boys had to get to the castle in the morning as the sun first shone on the gatehouse wall. This was where Juno had hidden Hercules' powers. For twenty minutes the superpowers glowed out of the stones around the arched entrance. At the same time the stones in front of Hercules' face crumbled. It was Juno's way of adding to his misery. He could look at his powers but not reach them. However, the boys could and every day Max or Finlay chose one of these superpowers to help them with their task. But those twenty minutes were all they had before the powers disappeared. There were three superpowers left – incredible-agility, deadly accuracy and courage.

Finlay was silent for a moment. 'I know,' he said at last. 'Let's tell your mum that I left my jumper there yesterday and need to get it back. We can run up there, get the superpower and get back in time to go to this dumb house. I'll come round now.'

'OK!' Max replied. 'See you in a few minutes!'

He shoved the ball in his pocket and hurried into the kitchen. 'Mum, Fin left his jumper at the castle yesterday and he's got to go and get it. Can I go with him?'

To his relief, his mum nodded. 'All right, but don't be long. Auntie Carol is coming here at nine-thirty with the girls.'

Max groaned inwardly. He'd been so busy thinking about how he and Finlay would do the task that he'd forgotten his mum had said his Auntie Carol and cousin Zoë and her friend Michelle were coming too. Zoë was thirteen years old. She was always making out she was really grown up and looking down her nose at him. *Still*, he thought, pushing thoughts of Zoë from his mind, *right now I have more important things to worry about — like choosing a superpower for the day!*

'I can't believe we've got to go to some ancient house,' Finlay said as they ran down the road together a few minutes later. 'I hope our plan works and we can get back soon to kill these man-eating birds! I wonder what they're going to be like?'

Max thought about the creatures Juno had conjured for them to face so far. They had all been terrifying *and* incredibly dangerous. He and Finlay had the scars to prove it. Every day one or other of them had been wounded. Max looked down at his two scars – both were in the shape of the superpower he had used for each task. They still hurt. Was he going to get wounded again that day? Or maybe worse . . .

'Look at this,' Finlay said, distracting Max from his worrying thoughts. Finlay pulled a red penknife out of his pocket. 'My dad got it free at the garage with some petrol and gave it to me. The knife bit is really small and blunt but there are some other good things on it like a tin-opener and a corkscrew. I thought it might come in useful today.'

'Um . . . how exactly?' Max said, not seeing exactly how a corkscrew or tin-opener could help them kill a flock of man-eating birds.

'Well, you never know,' Finlay said. 'It's got a screwdriver . . .'

'Great, so if they're robotic birds we can take them apart!' Max shook his head. 'Get real, Fin! What use is a screwdriver against man-eating birds?'

'Well, maybe the screwdriver isn't much use,' Finlay admitted, 'but there's this!' He flicked out a strange-looking gadget. 'My sister says it's for taking stones out of horses' feet.'

'Hey, cool! So when the birds are about to eat us we can ask them if they want a stone taking out of their feet,' Max said. 'Fin!'

'Oh, all right.' Finlay shoved the

penknife back in his pocket defensively. 'I just thought it might help.'

'What we need is a giant bird-eating cat,' Max said with feeling. 'Not a penknife!'

They ran up the path towards the ruined castle. 'So are you still going to choose accuracy as the superpower today?' Finlay asked. They'd talked about it the night before.

Max nodded. Being deadly accurate would be really cool, he'd be able to hit any target he wanted and never miss. That was bound to be a very useful ability to have that day. 'I'll be able to chuck things at the birds to kill them – stones, sticks . . .'

'A corkscrew?' Finlay said with a grin.

'Or maybe even a tin-opener.' Max

grinned back and they ran on.

The castle stood near the top of a hill. Its crumbling grey walls were surrounded by a dark moat. Max and Finlay ran over the bridge and clambered through the ruined gatehouse. As they emerged into the grassy castle keep, Max looked round. The sun was already shining on the gatehouse wall and three symbols were glowing in the stones around the archway – a leaping stag, an arrow and a lion.

'Hercules!' Max called.

'I am here,' a deep voice echoed across the keep.

Finlay and Max ran across the grass to the tower where stones had crumbled away to show the face of the superhero.

The very first time the boys had seen him he had looked incredibly ancient – his face carved in deep wrinkles, his skin dusty, his hair grey – but with every superpower the boys got back for him, he looked stronger and younger.

Hercules was very tall and he smiled down at the boys. 'You have come to try to complete another task.'

'Yes, we've got to kill a flock of man-eating birds today, haven't we?' Max said.

Hercules' golden eyes looked serious. 'The Man-Eating Birds of Stymphalia are extremely dangerous. They work together as a team to hunt down their prey. You must also work as a team if you are to defeat them. But you have proved in previous tasks that you are good at that.' He looked at Max. 'Have you decided which of my powers you will choose today?'

'Accuracy,' Max replied. Hercules nodded his approval. 'I'll get it now.' Max ran back to the gatehouse. Excitement beat through him. In just a few seconds he would get to be deadly accurate. The three symbols glowed in the stones, traced in lines of magical white fire. Stopping in front of the arched entrance, Max looked at the three pictures. Taking a deep breath, he placed his hand firmly on the arrow – the symbol for accuracy.

His fingers immediately started to tingle and he felt a fierce warmth flood into his hand. His head felt light as the

heat spread all the way down his arm,
through his body and into his toes. The
gatehouse stone turned cold and he
lifted his hand away. The superpower
was his!

CRASH!

A clap of thunder sounded. Max swung round. A very tall woman stood in the castle keep, a cloak of brown-grey feathers swirling around her, and her eyes glittering like laser beams.

Juno, Max thought with an icy chill of fear.

CHAPTER TWO

BULLSEYE!

Finlay raced across the keep to stand shoulder by shoulder with Max. They faced Juno together.

'So you have chosen accuracy!' the goddess snapped.

Max nodded.

A smile spread across Juno's face. 'It will not help you. You will *never* slay the Man-Eating Birds. They are incredibly intelligent and utterly vicious. To complete the task you must bring me *absolute proof* that you have killed all the birds in the flock. Are you ready to meet them?' She raised her hands.

'We can't fight them yet,' Max said quickly.

'Oh?' Juno raised an eyebrow.

'We . . .' Max's cheeks burned red. He knew how lame he was sounding. 'We've got to go out with my mum this morning.'

Juno smiled nastily. 'So, the mighty champion of Hercules must delay his task to go out with his *mother* to Haslemere House.'

Finlay stared. 'How did you know?'

'I am Juno,' she said simply. 'Well,

you needn't worry about coming back here to find the birds. They will find *you*.'

'No, Juno!' Hercules exclaimed.

Juno ignored him. She looked from Max to Finlay. 'To complete the task you must bring me absolute proof that you have killed them,' she said again. 'But no one must see them and not a . . .' she laughed, '*shred* of evidence must be left behind.'

'What do you mean?' Finlay started to ask.

But Juno was already clapping her hands together. There was a flash of lightning. The boys blinked in the bright light. When they opened their eyes she had gone.

'Weird!' Finlay said. 'I'd have thought

she would be pleased that we couldn't start the task until later. But by sending them to the house, she's made it easier for us.'

'No, boys!' Hercules shouted from the tower. 'Juno has not made it easier. The proof you need to bring is the –'

His voice was cut off as the stones around his face re-formed.

Max and Finlay found themselves staring at the tower wall.

'I wonder what he was going to say,' Max said slowly.

Finlay shrugged. 'I guess we're not going to find out.'

Max flexed his tingling fingers. 'I wonder what my power's like.'

Finlay looked round. 'I know. See if

you can hit the top of the tower with a stone.'

Max looked all the way up to the top of the tower, squinting against the sunlight. He picked up a pebble and weighed it in his hand. 'Which stone would you like me to hit?' he said.

Finlay grinned. 'That mouldy one in the very top row. The smallest one.'

Max drew back his arm and took aim. He felt a tingle run through his muscles – and almost without thinking, threw the pebble with a flick of his wrist. It sailed through the air – and bounced straight off the chosen stone.

'All right!' Finlay clapped. 'That's cool! Those birds won't stand a chance.'

Just then the church clock in the village struck half past nine. 'Help!' Max exclaimed. 'Mum said to be back by nine-thirty. Come on, Fin! We're going to be late!'

They reached Max's house just as a Land Rover drew up beside the gate.

Max's Auntie Carol waved at Max and Finlay from the driver's seat. 'Hello there,' she said, putting her window down. 'Are you two ready to go?'

'I think so,' Max replied. His cousin, Zoë, and her friend Michelle were in the back. Zoë ignored Max.

His auntie got out and opened the boot for them to climb in. 'In you get, boys!'

Max and Finlay climbed into the Land Rover. 'Hi, Zoë,' Max said, deciding to at least try and be friendly.

Zoë barely even glanced round. 'Yes,' she said briefly. She turned back to Michelle. 'So then she said . . .' she whispered something in Michelle's ears and the two girls gasped and giggled.

Max and Finlay sat down. Max had

to move a large denim bag from the seat he was going to sit on. As if she had eyes in the back of her head, Zoë immediately swung round. 'Don't touch my bag!' she snapped, reaching over the back of the seat and grabbing it from him.

'Sorry,' Max apologized.

'How could Max sit down without touching it?' Finlay pointed out fairly.

Michelle whispered something to Zoë. Both of them looked at him and giggled.

'What?' Finlay demanded, looking from one girl to the other.

'Is your hair always that messy?' Zoë sniggered.

Finlay frowned. 'Does your face always look like a bum?'

Zoë went red. She glared at him. 'Are
you always so immature?' She swung
back round. 'Ignore them,' she told
Michelle.

'Yes, please,' muttered Max,
exchanging looks with Finlay.

32

Max's mum and Auntie Carol got
into the front.

'All strapped in?' Auntie Carol asked
cheerily. 'Let's go, then. Haslemere
House, here we come — it's going to be
a lovely relaxing day out!'

Haslemere House was a large mansion
set in huge gardens.

'Where do you think the Man–Eating
Birds are?' Finlay said in a low voice to
Max as they got out of the Land Rover.

'I don't know.' A shiver ran through
Max.

Mrs Hayward smiled at them. 'Let's
go and have a look round the house.'

'Can Fin and I go and look round
the gardens instead, Mum?' Max asked.

But his mum shook her head. 'No,

come and see the house first. You can
see the gardens later.'

Max felt a wave of frustration, but
apart from just running off and getting
into trouble there was nothing much he
and Finlay could do. They reluctantly
followed the others up the path towards
the house entrance.

'Let's just get out as soon as we can,'
Finlay hissed.

Max nodded. There were Man-Eating
Birds out there. They had to find them
– before anyone else did!

The house was very grand, filled with
lots of pictures and old furniture and a
few suits of armour standing in the
corners. As Max's mum and his auntie
walked around, looking at all the
pictures, Zoë and Michelle walked

behind them, texting friends and
looking bored.

Every room seemed to lead to a new
room. Max began to feel as if they were
never going to get out of there.
Frustration buzzed through him. They
should be outside finding the
Man-Eating Birds!

He pushed his hands in his pocket
and felt the bouncy ball he'd been
playing with earlier. He took it out and
began bouncing it on the floor. As he
looked round the room he saw Zoë
and Michelle approaching a suit of
armour. One hand of the armour was
closed around a small double-headed
axe. The arm was raised, held in place
with a string tied to the wall. An idea
came to Max. If he could throw the

ball so that it landed on the string, the
arm would jerk just as the girls walked
past. Max grinned.

He nudged Finlay. 'Watch this!' he
said in a low voice.

He waited until the girls were walking towards the suit of armour.

Max threw the ball as hard as he could at the string. It hit it exactly where he had intended. The arm jerked up with the axe. The girls gasped in alarm and jumped back.

Max began to grin but his smile soon froze. As the arm of the armour fell back again the weight of it caused the string to break. The axe fell away from the armour and landed with a clatter on the stone floor. Meanwhile the bouncy ball rebounded off the string, flying upwards like a jet-propelled missile.

'Oh no!' gasped Fin, staring in horror as the ball hit the ceiling and came shooting back down, whacking into the suit of armour's helmet. The visor fell down with a clang and made all the visitors turn round and stare in shock.

'Max!' Mrs Hayward exclaimed in horror. 'Whatever do you think you are doing?'

CHAPTER THREE

IN TROUBLE . . .

Max turned to face his mum. 'Sorry!'

Mrs Hayward looked extremely cross.
'Honestly, Max! What were you
thinking of? Playing with a ball in here
of all places!'

A member of staff who worked at the
house came hurrying into the room.
'What's happened?' he asked.

'We're terribly sorry,' Auntie Carol

started to say. 'There's been an accident . . .'

The man grunted grumpily. 'Now I'll have to take it down to the workshop to mend it.'

Mrs Hayward looked embarrassed. 'I'm so sorry about it.' She turned to Max. 'Maybe you and Finlay should go outside after all.'

Max could have punched the air in delight. *Result!*

'Can we go outside too?' Zoë asked eagerly.

'All right,' Auntie Carol said. 'There's a maze outside and several aviaries full of birds.' She looked at the leaflet about the house that she had picked up at the entrance. 'It says here there's also baby lambs and foals in the stables, peacocks in the gardens and an emu paddock beside the maze.'

'Let's go and see the foals,' Michelle said to Zoë.

'See you later, Mum!' Max exclaimed, not wanting to waste another second inside.

He and Finlay ran out through the house and down the steps.

'We got out!' Finlay exclaimed, jumping down the last three steps in one go. 'Let's find us some man-eating birds!' He looked at the gardens spread out before him. 'Which way should we go?'

'It says aviaries that way!' Max said, pointing at a sign. 'Let's try down there. That's where birds are kept.'

They set off down a gravel path that led between two tall hedges. It was quite a long path. At the very end of it there was a courtyard. On one side was a long, low building with the word *Workshop* on the door. On the other side were cages of tiny birds. They swooped around the cages, perching on branches and singing sweetly.

'If they're the man-eating birds I'm *so* not frightened,' Finlay said.

Max sniggered. 'Those birds couldn't even eat a little toe, let alone a whole man!'

Suddenly there was an ear-splitting shriek from just outside the courtyard.

Max's heart thudded in his chest. 'What was that?' he whispered.

Finlay gulped. 'I don't know, but I'm guessing it's these little birds' big brother – their *very* big brother!'

A second savage screech rent the air. It seemed to be coming from the other side of the courtyard where there was an archway and a sign above it that said: *This way to the Emu Paddock and Maze.*

Max took a deep breath. 'Come on!'

They walked through the archway
that led out of the courtyard and
stopped dead. To one side of them was
a large maze made out of thick green
hedges and on the other side of them
was a fenced field. A sign on the gate
said: *Emu Paddock.*

'If they're emus, I'm a gorilla,' Max
hissed.

Nine giant birds with huge curved
beaks were standing in a circle in the
centre of the field. Each of them
looked like a cross between a dinosaur
and a bird. They had long scaly legs,
dirty hooked claws on their feet,
beady red eyes, small leathery wings
and round bodies covered in jet-black
feathers.

'What do you think they've done

with the real emus?' Finlay whispered
nervously to Max.

Max gulped. 'Eaten them?'

Finlay suddenly noticed something.
'They've got something in there with
them!' he said in alarm. 'They're
surrounding it!'

He and Max hurried to the fence.
A peacock was trapped in the centre of
the circle of birds. It was crouching
down, looking absolutely terrified. The
monster birds shrieked triumphantly.
One of the birds lifted its long curved
beak high above the peacock's head.
Opening its mouth it gave an evil
screech and began to swing its beak
downwards.

'No!' Max yelled, unable to watch the
peacock being killed.

The Man-Eating Birds swung round. Spotting the boys, they let out savage cries and, leaving the peacock, they began to stalk quickly across the paddock towards Max and Finlay. The peacock scrambled away with a relieved cry. The birds began to move faster.

Their red eyes were fixed hungrily on the two boys.

Their beaks opened.

'Quick, Max!' Finlay exclaimed in horror. 'Run!'

CHAPTER FOUR

IN THE MAZE

Max and Finlay tore away from the paddock. Behind them the birds shrieked. Max could hear the pounding of their heavy taloned feet as they charged across the grass. Thank goodness their wings weren't big enough for them to be able to fly. He glanced round desperately. There was still the fence. Maybe that would stop them . . .

Crash! The leading bird smacked like a Sherman tank into the fence. The planks of wood cracked and broke. The other birds began slashing at the wood with their beaks, tearing off great chunks and chucking them out of the way as they ripped the fence apart.

Finlay ducked to avoid a half plank of wood as it thudded into the ground beside him. 'Which way?' he shouted to Max.

Max looked round. 'Let's go through the courtyard!' he gasped.

But as they turned towards the courtyard, three birds charged through the hole in the fence and headed them off. The birds stopped by the courtyard entrance. They stretched out their heads and necks, their razor-sharp beaks opening.

The remaining birds spread out and began striding purposefully towards them, their beady eyes fixed on the two boys.

Max and Finlay looked round. Where could they go? The birds were closing in on all sides.

'What are we going to do, Fin?' Max said.

Finlay looked around. 'Let's go into the maze!'

He and Max ran towards the maze. The birds stalked after them; they walked together in a group, their red eyes gleaming. Max had a sudden, horrible feeling that he and Finlay were being made to go exactly where the birds wanted them to go. But what else could they do? The birds had them surrounded!

Reaching a sign that said *Entrance*, Max and Finlay ran into the maze. On either side of them the hedges grew up thick and strong.

'So what now?' Max heard a screech behind him and knew with a horrible sinking feeling in his stomach that the birds had entered the maze too.

'We've got to lose them and then get out of here!' Finlay panted.

Max nodded. 'What about killing them?'

'Let's just stop them from killing us first!' said Finlay.

They reached a turning in the maze. 'Let's go right!' Max decided.

They took the right but within seconds had run straight into a dead end.

'Wrong way!' groaned Finlay. 'We'll have to go back!'

'But what about the birds?' Max demanded. 'They might be there!'

As he spoke an evil shriek came from just the other side of the hedge. Max

and Finlay both jumped in alarm.
'Argh!'

The bird gave another shriek and
began slashing at the hedge with its
beak. 'We can't stay here!' Finlay gasped.
'Come on!'

He and Max charged back down the
path, their trainers kicking up gravel,
their breath coming in ragged gasps.
They came to a leafy crossroads. Birds
ran towards them from both the right
and the left.

'Quick!' yelled Max. He led the way
down the only possible route – straight
ahead!

Another bird burst into view at the
far end of the path. Its curved beak
snapped open with triumph as it saw
them.

'Two behind us and one ahead,' Finlay panted as he and Max screeched to a halt.

Max's thoughts raced. What could they do? Which way should they go? He could hear the birds coming up behind them and he made a decision. 'This way!' he exclaimed, charging straight *towards* the giant bird in front of them.

'Max!' Finlay shouted in alarm.

'Trust me! It's our only chance,' Max yelled back. His heart pounded. There *had* to be another path leading off along here; surely the hedged-in passage was too long for there *not* to be one? At the far end, the monster bird's eyes glowed a darker red and narrowed

as it began to stalk eagerly to meet
them.

Max could hear Finlay's feet tearing
over the gravel right behind him. Sweat
prickled down Max's back. If he was
wrong about this, then he was killing
Fin as well as himself . . .

Suddenly, to his right, he saw the opening that he'd been hoping for – another route leading off deeper into the maze. 'Here!' he exclaimed and, skidding to a halt, he grabbed hold of Finlay's arm and bundled him down the new path.

The monster birds were moving too fast to turn in time. They crashed into each other. Screeches of rage and feathers filled the air.

'Yes!' Finlay shouted, punching the air in triumph.

'Come on!' Max urged. He knew that any head start they could get on the birds was vital. The path forked off left and right, he chose right – just as another bird's beak smashed through the foliage, tearing for the flesh of their arms.

They both dodged out of the way just in time.

Ignoring the stitch blazing in his side, Max set off again at his fastest run. There were so many different pathways. He'd never been in such a thick maze and there seemed to be birds everywhere. Just one of them could kill both him and Fin!

He took a right. Left. Right again. Another left.

And then suddenly they were in a larger space, a perfect square boxed in by hedges. In the middle of it was a high wooden platform. Steps led up to the platform and there was a railing all the way round the edge. A round metal sign screwed on to a wooden post set in a heavy base said: *Centre of Maze*.

'We've reached the middle!' Max
gasped.

Finlay panted for breath and listened.
'Where are the birds?' They could hear
distant screeches further away in the
maze passageways but no sound of birds
nearby. 'Maybe we've lost them. I know,
let's get up on that platform. We'll be
able to see over the hedges from there!'
Finlay clambered up the steps. 'Hey,
Max! You can see the whole maze!'
he hissed.

Max followed him. Finlay was right.
Standing up on the wooden platform
he could see out over the whole maze
with its network of linked passageways,
thick hedges and dead ends. The breath
caught in his throat. Four birds were
stalking along a pathway quite near to

the centre. Even worse, another four
birds were approaching from the
opposite direction. Their eyes gleamed
and they cawed harshly as if they
were talking to each other, planning
and plotting. Shivers ran down Max's

spine. There was no way he and Finlay could get out past them, at least not if they wanted to stay alive.

'Fin! What are we going to do?' he said. 'We're trapped!'

CHAPTER FIVE

TRAPPED!

'Hang on!' Finlay exclaimed. 'Look, Max!'

He pulled Max round and pointed at a narrow overgrown path on the other side of the centre of the maze that led between two hedges all the way to the outside. There was a green gate at the end with a large sign on it.

'Escape Gate,' Max read out. Relief

surged through him. 'It's an exit, so people don't have to get out by going all the way back through the maze! Come on, Fin. We can get out that way!' He began scrambling down the steps.

Finlay was about to follow him when he saw something that sent his heart plummeting into his trainers. A Man-Eating Bird was walking past the gate on the outside of the maze. As he watched, it turned round and walked back. It was obviously guarding the escape gate. 'Wait, Max!' he hissed. 'There's a bird there!'

Max climbed back up the steps and looked. The bird had the meanest eyes and the longest beak of all the birds he had seen. Glancing round, Max saw that

the other eight birds were stalking
horribly near to the pathway that led
into the centre of the maze now. They
had their heads outstretched and kept
stopping every few paces, as if
listening to guess where the boys
might be.

If they came into the centre he and Finlay wouldn't stand a chance.

If only there was some way I could use my superpower to stop the birds from coming into the centre, Max thought desperately. *If I could just get them to go away from here then maybe we could figure out how to get past that one guard bird at the exit.* But how could he possibly do that? The only thing that would make the birds go away would be if they thought he and Finlay weren't there any more . . .

Max's eyes fell on the chunky gravel at the base of the platform and an idea exploded into his mind. He hurried down the steps and grabbed a huge handful of stones.

'What are you doing?' Finlay demanded.

'I've had an idea,' Max answered, climbing back up. He carefully chucked a large stone so that it landed on the gravel path next to the one the birds were walking along. It fell exactly where he wanted. Then he threw another slightly further along and then another and another so that it sounded like someone's feet creeping along the gravel. Every stone landed perfectly.

The birds' heads shot up and they looked towards the hedge.

The leading bird gave a screech and turned round. It headed towards the path where the gravel was landing.

'It's working!' Finlay whispered in delight as all the birds began to stalk into the pathway that led away from the centre. 'They must think we're over there!'

Max threw some stones in the opposite direction. The birds stopped, looking confused. Half of them headed one way and half the other. But the important thing was that they weren't heading back to the centre!

'Brilliant! If we can just get past the bird by the escape gate we'll be out!' Finlay said. 'If only we had a weapon to help us.'

'A sword or axe would be good,' Max agreed. 'But we've got nothing.'

Finlay's eyes fell on the sign below them. It was made of two thin circles of metal screwed on to either side of the wooden post, which had been placed in a heavy metal base. His eyes lit up. 'Actually, maybe we have!' He scrambled down the steps and fished his penknife out of his pocket.

'What are you doing?' Max asked in astonishment.

Finlay didn't answer. Flicking the screwdriver out of the penknife he began to unscrew one of the metal circles. Within seconds he had taken it off the post and was unscrewing the second one. 'Here!' he said, holding up the flat metal discs in triumph. 'I knew my screwdriver would come in useful! These are perfect! You can use them like throwing discs.' He pretended to throw one. 'Bet you could easily cut the bird's head off with one of these and your super-accuracy.' He climbed back up the steps. 'You can chuck it from here!'

Max took one of the discs from him and looked towards the escape gate. Would it work? The Man-Eating Bird was standing still now, just behind the gate. Its red eyes were gleaming evilly. Max's fingers felt the sharpness

of the edge. Fin was right. If he threw the disc hard enough and it hit its target . . .

He assessed the distance from the platform to the bird and adjusted his fingers on the metal disc. It would be just like throwing a frisbee – though admittedly a metal, chopping-your-head-off kind of frisbee.

The bird let out a savage screech.

Max glanced round and saw the other bird monsters still hunting through the maze. They had to get out of there, and tackling one bird was better than meeting eight!

'OK,' he said determinedly. 'I'll do it.'

He brought the disc up to his chest, turned sideways on and then threw it as hard as he could. The disc whizzed

through the air. Max caught his breath.
It was going to hit the bird's neck dead
on target . . .

'Yes!' Fin started to say in triumph,
but at the very last moment the bird

spotted the disc. With a furious screech, it jerked its head out of the way. The disc reached the point exactly where Max had been aiming but the bird was no longer there! Giving a terrible shrieking cry, the bird pushed open the gate and began to stalk down the pathway towards the centre.

'It knows we're here now!' Finlay gasped. He shoved the other disc into Max's hand. 'You've got one more chance! You've got to get it this time, Max, before it gets us!'

'But what if it ducks again, Fin!' Max exclaimed.

Finlay muttered to himself. 'Think. Think.' He turned to Max. 'OK, we need to distract it, so it isn't looking at you or the disc, is that right?'

'Yes! But how are we going to do that?' Max demanded. 'We haven't got anything to distract it with!'

Finlay looked at him grimly. 'Yes we have! Me!'

CHAPTER SIX

THUNK!

Max stared at Finlay. 'We can't use you to distract the bird, Fin!'

'Wanna bet?' Finlay said. He jumped down the steps. 'Just don't miss with the disc this time, Max, or I'll be bird food!'

'No, Fin. It's too dangerous!' Max protested. 'If the bird moves again and I miss, the bird might get you! Wait . . .!'

But Finlay was already running towards the escape-gate pathway so that the bird could see him. 'Hey, you big roast chicken!' he shouted at it. 'Can't get me!' He jumped up and down, waving his arms and pulling a face. 'Over here, bird-brain!'

With a screech the bird broke into a run. It raced into the centre of the maze, eyes blazing; hungry drool dripping from its savage beak. Finlay turned and raced across the gravel. The monster bird lowered its head and charged after him, its vicious beak opening wide.

Max didn't stop to think. The bird's neck was stretched out as it raced past him. Taking aim, he threw the disc as hard as he could. It spun through the air in a silver blur.

Thunk!

Max's super-accurate judgement was perfect. The disc sliced straight through the monster bird's long neck. The bird's head catapulted upwards. As it spun around in the air it disappeared, and the

body suddenly collapsed to the ground.
Max caught his breath, expecting to see
blood or goo start pouring out, but
nothing happened and then suddenly
the end of the neck started to move.
A much smaller beak popped out.

'What . . .' the word died on Max's
lips. He stared at the bird's body in
horror. The neck twitched and then
another head appeared. Oh no!

'It's like the river monster we fought!'
Finlay shouted in alarm, backing away
from it. 'It's growing new heads!'

'No,' Max said quickly, his eyes on the
emerging head. 'Look! It's different!'

The whole of the bird's body shook
and suddenly a different type of bird
wriggled its way out through the neck.
It still had long legs, a long neck and

short wings but apart from that
everything about it was different. It
had a small head, brown eyes, pale grey
feathers and a delicate pointed beak.
It gave a surprised squawk.

'It's an emu!' Max said in astonishment.

'So the monster birds didn't eat them!
It must be part of Juno's magic,' Finlay
gasped. 'She's enchanted the emus to be
the Man-Eating Birds.'

'And if we chop the heads off the
Man-Eating Birds, they turn back into
their emu shape,' Max said, looking at
the now very flat skin of the monster
bird lying on the floor.

'Guess we'd better get chopping,
then,' Finlay said, going over to the
skin. He poked it with his foot. 'We'll
need to take this back with us. It must

be what Juno meant about taking absolute proof that we've killed all the birds.'

Max climbed down from the platform and looked at the skin. It was slightly damp but drying out fast. 'Let's leave it here,' he said, pushing it under the platform with his foot. 'We can come back for it later. Right now we should get out of here and find some weapons before the other birds come looking for us!'

The disc that Max had used to chop off the bird's head had ended up in the top of one of the hedges. Max tried to shake it down, but it was stuck fast. In the distance there was the sound of a shriek.

'Come on!' Finlay said quickly.

'We can find some other weapons. There's that workshop in the courtyard. There's bound to be something in there that we can use.'

Listening to the distant shrieks of the birds in the rest of the maze, they ran thankfully down the path to the escape gate.

'I hope no one else decides to go into the maze,' said Max.

Finlay nodded. 'We'd better get some weapons quickly!'

They began to run towards the courtyard but as they did so, Zoë and Michelle came walking through the archway!

'Oh no!' Max exclaimed to Finlay.

'Where are you going?' Finlay demanded, running up to them.

'To the maze,' Michelle answered.

'Not that it's anything to do with you!' Zoë said.

'You can't go in there!' Max told her.

Zoë raised her eyebrows. 'Says who?'

'You just can't,' Max insisted. He stepped in front of her.

'Get out of my way, Max!' Zoë said, looking irritated.

Max looked at Finlay. Other people weren't supposed to know about their tasks, but this was an emergency. 'There are Man-Eating Birds in there!' he said.

'Oh, grow up,' Zoë told him witheringly. 'Come on, Michelle. Just ignore them.'

The girls pushed past the boys.

'This looks like a way in,' Zoë said, spotting the escape gate that the boys had left open. 'Come on!' She and Michelle set off through the gate.

'No, Zoë!' Max yelled. He began to run towards the gate as the girls disappeared down the path. 'Come back . . .'

His words were cut off by a piercing scream!

CHAPTER SEVEN

CHASED BY A BIRD

Max felt like a bucket of icy water had been tipped over his head.

Finlay turned pale. 'They must have met the birds!' he gasped.

There was another loud scream and then to Max's astonishment and relief the two girls came running out of the maze as fast as they could.

'A huge bird!' Zoë gasped. 'It's after us!'

A bird came running out of the maze, its light-grey feathery wings flapping, its brown eyes confused.

Max and Finlay stared. It wasn't a Man-Eating Bird. It was the emu!

'Argh!' the girls shrieked as the emu ran towards them.

Zoë dropped her rucksack in her panic and she and Michelle raced away into the courtyard.

Max and Finlay looked at each other and burst out laughing.

The emu stopped and looked round, then trotted back into its field, carefully picking its way over the broken fence. Once there it gave a relieved squawk.

Finlay grinned at Max. 'Come on, we'd better get some weapons and try to kill the real Man-Eating Birds before anyone else comes along!' he said.

To the boys' disappointment, although the workshop door was open, the tools were all locked away in a cabinet. Lying on the side was the suit of armour that Max had damaged earlier.

The double-headed axe was beside it. 'We could use this,' Max said, grabbing it.

'Yeah,' Finlay agreed. He looked around but the only other things in the workshop were a large empty paint pot, a plastic carrier bag and an old pair of pliers. He took them all just in case they came in useful.

They ran back to the maze. Max couldn't go as fast as before because the axe was heavy. On the way there, Finlay spotted Zoë's bag. 'We could use this to put the birds' skins inside once we've killed them.'

'*If* we kill them,' Max said, his heart beating fast. Now they were near the maze again he was beginning to feel very nervous. 'Which way shall we go in?' he asked, lowering his voice as he looked at the maze.

'Through the escape gate,' Finlay whispered. 'I reckon our best chance is to get to the centre and then lure the birds in there. As they come into the centre you can be lying in wait and chop their heads off with the axe.'

Max nodded. It was as good a plan as any, though right then he'd have given anything to be able to run away in the opposite direction!

They crept as quietly as they could down the path. Scalps prickling, muscles tensed, they listened for the slightest sound as they stepped into the centre of the maze.

'All clear,' Finlay breathed.

The skin of the bird they had killed

was still under the bench but it seemed to have dried up and shrunk.

Finlay went over with Zoë's rucksack. He dumped the paint pot and pliers on the ground and then, kneeling down, he emptied the contents of the rucksack into the carrier bag he'd found in the workshop: a hairbrush, a magazine, a bag of make-up and a letter with hearts drawn all over it that was written in pink writing. The first line caught his eyes:

To Jake, my cutest big huggy-bear

His eyes jumped to the last line:

Love and cuddles, from your little snuggly squoogles, Zoë XXXXXXXXXXXXXX

For a moment, Finlay forgot about the Man-Eating Birds! A grin spread across his face. 'Hey, Max! Look at this!' he hissed. 'It's a soppy love letter from Zoë to someone she calls her big huggy bear!'

Max looked at it and pulled a face. 'Yuck!'

Finlay grinned and shoved the letter into his pocket. Then he bent forward to pick up the Man-Eating Bird skin and put it in the bag. But the skin was so dry and thin now, that as he picked it up his fingers tore straight through it and it broke into pieces. Every time Finlay tried to pick up one of the pieces his fingers damaged the skin some more. He exclaimed in frustration as the skin started disintegrating.

'Stop, Fin!' Max whispered in alarm. 'If we lose *any* of the pieces, we'll have failed the task. Don't you remember Juno saying that to complete the task we must take back *every shred*? I bet this is her way of making the task harder!'

Finlay groaned. 'Of course! No

wonder Juno was happy for us to do
the task further away from the castle.
She knew it would be more difficult
for us to get back with every bit of
the monster skins.'

'Here, let me try picking up the bits,'
Max said. 'Maybe the superpower will
help.' He bent over and picked up a bit
of the skin on the floor. His fingers
tingled; the superpower allowed Max to
judge with absolute accuracy how hard
he could hold the skin without it
tearing. With the precision of a brain
surgeon he neatly folded the bit of skin
and placed it carefully in Zoë's bag.

'Wow!' Finlay said. 'That's cool!'

Max carefully placed every shred of
the monster skin into the bag and
straightened up. 'One skin ready to take

home. Now all we need to do is kill the other eight birds.' He picked up the axe. 'I guess we should really fold their skins straight away, before they dry out. That will make it easier and quicker.'

'Hang on. You can't kill the birds *and* fold the skins up at the same time,' Finlay pointed out. 'And anyway, the birds might trample over the skins while you're trying to kill them.'

'So what can we do?' Max frowned. 'I have to fold the skins because I've got the superpower.'

'Then it looks like I'm going to have to kill the birds,' Finlay declared.

Max stared at him. 'But you haven't got the superpower, Fin. What if you miss?'

Finlay looked grim. 'I guess I'd better

not.' He stood up and went to the steps. 'I'll go and see if I can see where the birds are —'

But just as he spoke there was a piercing shriek and a Man-Eating Bird stepped into the centre of the maze. It stopped and looked at them, its red eyes

burning; its dagger-like claws gripping the ground. Seeing the boys it began to charge excitedly towards them, its wings flapping; its cruel beak open.

'The axe, Fin!' Max shouted. He chucked the axe at Finlay, who caught it.

Finlay didn't stop to think. Gripping it tightly, he raced to meet the bird!

CHAPTER EIGHT

INTO BATTLE!

The Man-Eating Bird bore down on Finlay. Finlay swung the axe up, dodged to the side and brought it down as hard as he could.

Thunk!

The axe chopped through the monster's neck, cutting off its shrieking victory cry.

'You did it!' Max shouted to Finlay.

Just as before, the head vanished as it
flew through the air. The body
collapsed to the floor and a few
moments later, an emu was wriggling
its way out.

Finlay stared at it, torn between shock
that he'd done it and delight. But he
didn't have time to stand still for long.
The Man-Eating Bird's shrieks had
attracted the attention of the other birds
and even as Max began to quickly and
precisely gather up the skin, two more
birds burst into the centre of the maze.

'Hi-yaah!' Finlay yelled, charging to
meet them.

Thunk! Thwack!

Two more heads flew into the air.
A fourth bird appeared. Finlay swung
towards it, but as he did so, it ducked

and he lost his balance. The weight of the axe dragged him forward as the axe's head bit into the ground.

'Finlay!' Max yelled in alarm as the bird swung round and raised its beak over Finlay's head. Grabbing the first thing that came to hand – the large empty paint pot from the workshop – Max chucked it at the bird. It landed perfectly on the bird's head. The bird shook its head furiously, but Finlay had seen his chance. Yanking the axe out of the ground he swung it through the bird's neck.

'Four down!' he yelled to Max as the bird collapsed. 'Four to go!'

Trying to herd the emus away down to the escape gate, Max began to fold up the skins. It was hard to concentrate with so much going on around him but he kept his head down and focused on folding up the disintegrating skins. They had to get every last shred of them back to Juno or they would fail the whole task. Hearing another thunk, he looked up.

'Five down!' Finlay shouted triumphantly as another bird fell to the ground. 'Just three more!'

'And here they come!' Max shouted as the three remaining Man-Eating Birds raced into the maze. They screeched as they saw Finlay with the axe. He hesitated for a second, unsure which one to go for first.

In that second of hesitation they surrounded him. Their eyes gleamed as they raised their necks. Max saw Finlay

look round in alarm. He couldn't
possibly get all three at once. The birds
opened their beaks . . .

Max grabbed the pair of heavy metal
pliers, turned on the spot and in the
same movement chucked the pliers at
one of the bird's heads. It hit the bird
with a heavy clunk. The bird slumped
to the ground. Finlay quickly chopped
its head off.

The other two birds shrieked in fury.
Finlay leapt towards one, the axe
swinging straight for its neck.

At the same moment the other bird
began to run at Max. He looked round
desperately. What could he use as a
weapon? Suddenly he saw the wooden
post they had unscrewed the metal discs
from earlier and picked it up. Running
forward to meet the bird he swung it
upside down so the heavy metal base
was pointing upwards. The bird bore
down on him, flapping its wings. It
looked huge – enormous. Its savage
beak sliced downwards.

Using all his strength, Max shoved the
signpost upwards into the bird's open
mouth. His aim was perfect. The bird's
beak closed on the metal base with a

loud clunk. For a moment its mouth was so full of metal that it couldn't do anything, but then within seconds, it had ripped through the wood, shearing off the metal base. Spitting out the metal and wood, it shrieked in fury and slashed at Max again. Max dodged back in alarm but he wasn't quite quick enough. The bird's beak caught the top of his arm.

He yelled in pain. The bird raised its head to strike again. Heart pounding, Max grabbed the wooden post from the ground. It was the only possible weapon to hand. What could he do? He looked down and saw the bird's taloned webbed foot just centimetres away from his own. The bird's beak was already stabbing down towards him.

Max ducked and in the same movement threw the wooden stake through the webbing on the bird's foot. It speared through and stuck in the ground.

The bird screeched and tried to pull its foot away but it was pinned fast. 'Fin!' Max yelled. 'The axe!'

Finlay raced over, panting, and threw the axe at Max. Max caught it perfectly and cut straight through the bird's neck. The head shot past him and vanished. The body slumped to the floor. He'd done it! He'd killed the final bird!

He looked up and saw Finlay standing red-faced and panting a few metres away.

'We did it,' Max said shakily.

'Just,' said Finlay, swallowing.

They looked round. After all the
screeching and shrieking the centre of
the maze seemed suddenly very quiet.
The emus had disappeared down the
exit path and they were on their own
with just the few remaining skins.

Max drew a trembling breath and
examined the wound on his arm.
Blood was seeping out of it. 'That
was a tough task.'

'The toughest yet,' Fin agreed.

Max looked at him with respect.
'It took real guts to fight all those birds
like that, Fin. You didn't even
have a superpower to help you.'

Finlay grinned. 'I'm just glad my
guts didn't end up splattered all over
the floor!'

Max grinned back and carefully

picked up the remaining skins. He folded them and put them in the rucksack. 'That's all of them,' he said.

'We just need to get them back to Juno now,' Finlay agreed.

Max frowned as he saw a problem. 'Um . . . Fin, how are we going to persuade Zoë to let us use her bag on the way home? She wouldn't even let me touch it before.'

A grin spread over Finlay's face. 'A-ha!' he said, pulling the letter out of his pocket. 'We use this.'

'Is that the soppy love letter?' Max said.

Finlay nodded. 'A soppy love letter I'm betting she doesn't want your aunt or your mum to see.'

Max stared at him. 'So you mean we

say to her we'll show it to them if she doesn't let us use her bag?'

Finlay grinned. 'Yep! Let's see how she likes that!'

Max grinned back. 'Cool!'

They ran out of the maze. Finlay's mum and auntie were walking out of the courtyard with Zoë and Michelle.

'A great big bird?' Max heard his mum saying. 'You mean one of the emus!'

'It must have escaped from its paddock,' Auntie Carol said. She looked across at the paddock. 'Yes, look, the fence is broken!' She smiled. 'Honestly, girls, I can't believe you two were so scared of an emu.'

'It ran towards us,' Michelle said.

'And the boys had told us that there was a man-eating bird in the maze,' Zoë said. 'So . . . So . . .'

Auntie Carol and Max's mum burst out laughing.

'A man-eating bird!' Max's mum

exclaimed. 'Oh, Zoë! How old are you? Surely you didn't believe a silly story like that!'

Zoë and Michelle both looked a bit embarrassed.

Max grinned at Finlay. 'Cos you'd never really get a real man-eating bird in a maze, would you!' he muttered.

His mum noticed them. 'I hear you two have been scaring the girls,' she called, but from her smile Max could tell she wasn't cross. 'Man-eating birds! What will you think of next!' She headed towards the maze. 'Well, let's see what this maze is like, then.'

Zoë's eyes had fallen on her bag. 'What are you doing with that?' she hissed, hurrying over to the boys. 'That's *my* bag!'

'Can we borrow it, please?' Finlay asked.

'No way!' Zoë said, trying to snatch it off him.

Finlay whisked it out of her reach. 'I think you meant to say yes,' he told her.

'No, I didn't,' Zoë retorted.

'Oh yes you did!' Finlay pulled the letter out of his pocket. 'Cos if you said no we might just have to show this to your mum and Max's mum. Right, Max?'

Max grinned and nodded. 'Yep, that's right.' He looked at Zoë. 'Little snuggly squoogles . . .'

Zoë gasped and her face turned as red as a tomato. 'You went through my bag! You . . . you . . .'

'What's it to be?' Finlay interrupted. 'We get to use your bag for today –

you can have it and the letter back this evening – or we show the letter now?'

Zoë glanced round to where Michelle and the two mums were about to go into the maze. 'Oh, OK, then,' she said through gritted teeth. 'You keep the bag, but I want it back by this evening.'

'Deal,' Max said quickly.

'And don't do anything gross with it!' she added.

'It's OK,' said Fin, grinning. 'We only want it to keep some dead bird skins safe.'

'Ha, ha, you are just *so* funny, Finlay.' Zoë gave them a furious look and then turned and stomped off.

Max's mum stopped by the maze entrance. 'Are you coming in as well, boys?'

Max and Finlay shook their heads firmly.

'I've had enough of mazes for one day,' Max muttered to Finlay.

'I've got my pocket money with me,' Finlay said. 'Let's go and get an ice cream!'

CHAPTER NINE

BACK TO THE CASTLE

After lunch, Auntie Carol drove them
all home. To Max's relief, his mum said
he and Finlay could go up to the castle.

They raced up the path. As they ran
over the bridge there was a loud bang
and the bag suddenly got lighter on
Max's back. He opened the top. 'The
skins have gone!' he exclaimed.

They hurried in through the

gatehouse. Juno was standing in the middle of the keep. She looked furious. 'You have completed the task!'

The boys stopped warily by the gatehouse wall. 'Yes,' Max said.

'Bah!' Juno spat.

Max felt a warm swirling sensation in his chest and a flood of golden light burst out of him. He felt dizzy. The superpower had gone! It streamed across the keep and hit the inner wall of the tower opposite.

Almost immediately the bricks crumbled. The boys saw Hercules look out.

'You did it!' Hercules exclaimed triumphantly. 'My superpower has returned to me!'

They raced over to him. His face was

looking less lined and his eyes glowed golden. 'You killed the Stymphalian Birds and brought back their skins!' he said. 'How did you do it?'

'It wasn't easy,' Max said, shivering at the memory. 'We had to use an axe and a disc and hide in a maze . . .' He and Finlay quickly told Hercules what they'd done.

Hercules smiled from one to the

other. 'You used all your strengths. You worked as a team, battling side by side, trusting each other. You did very well.'

'Those birds were mean!' Finlay said. 'It was the hardest task yet.'

Juno strode towards them, her eyes flashing fire. 'You will not be saying that tomorrow! In the morning, you must fetch me the three golden apples of the gods. It is a task that requires great courage and wisdom. You must solve a riddle to help you steal the apples. Make one mistake and . . .' she looked from one to the other, 'a fate *worse* than death awaits.'

'We won't make a mistake!' Finlay told her.

'No,' Max said, moving so they were standing side by side. 'We're going to get Hercules another of his superpowers back.'

'I doubt it very much,' Juno sneered.

'You have been wrong evey day so far, Juno,' Hercules said in his deep voice.

'Silence!' Juno clapped her hands and the stones closed over his face. She looked at the boys. 'I hope you like dogs!'

Laughing evilly she clapped her hands again. There was a flash of lightning and a thunderclap and she disappeared.

A hawk swooped upwards into the air. 'What do you think she meant about dogs?' Max said slowly.

'Something tells me she's not talking about a Labrador,' Finlay replied, with a shaky grin. 'Anyway, I'm more worried about this fate worse than death she was talking about!'

Max lifted his chin. 'Well, whatever Juno's got planned, we'll complete the task tomorrow,' he said determinedly.

'We will! Just two more tasks to go!' Finlay said. 'Then Hercules will be free!'

'And Juno will be sorry!' Max declared. 'We'll show her!'

Overhead the hawk cried out and circled like a dark, defiant shadow in the sky.

ABOUT THE AUTHOR

ALEX CLIFF LIVES IN A VILLAGE IN
LEICESTERSHIRE, NEXT DOOR TO FIN AND
JUST DOWN THE ROAD FROM MAX, BUT
UNFORTUNATELY THERE IS NO CASTLE ON
THE OUTSKIRTS OF THE VILLAGE.
ALEX'S HOME IS FILLED WITH TWO
CHILDREN AND TWO LARGE AND VERY
SLOBBERY PET MONSTERS.

WILL MAX AND FIN SAVE HERCULES IN TIME?

CAN THEY TAKE ON A MASSIVE THREE-HEADED HOUND?

DID YOU KNOW?

Hercules lived in Ancient Greece. He was the son of a woman named Alcmene and the god Zeus. When Hercules was a baby he could fight snakes with his bare hands! The labours he had to complete were originally set for him by his cousin Eurystheus, King of Mycenae.

THE STYMPHALIAN BIRDS

These were vicious man-eating birds whose beaks could penetrate a man's armour. Even their feathers could kill so they used them as missiles. They lived in a dangerous and well-protected swamp in Arcadia. To reach the birds Hercules had to make a huge noise. The sound disturbed the birds from their hiding place in the trees and Hercules shot them down with a bow and arrow as they took flight.

YOUR
SUPER POWERS
QUEST

YOU NEED:
2 players
2 counters
1 dice
and nerves of steel!

YOU MUST:
Collect all **seven** superpowers and save Hercules, who has been trapped in the castle by the evil goddess, Juno. All you have to do is roll the dice and follow the steps on the books – try not to land on Juno's rock or one of the monsters!

JOIN THE QUEST!
COLLECT ALL 7 BOOKS AND PLAY THE SUPERPOWERS GAME

START

1 You need a **SUPERPOWER** to save Hercules, off you go!

2 You've got today's power – strength! **MOVE FORWARD THREE ROCKS**

7 **YOWSERS!** You've left the hammer behind. MISS A GO

3 **OH NO!** You've landed on Juno's rock. Back to the start!

6 **RUN FASTER!** It's getting closer. **ROLL AGAIN**

8 **GO!** You're only six powers from saving Hercules. GO TO THE NEXT QUEST!

4 **EEK!** Time is running out, but you can't move until you roll a three.

5 **YIKES!** You must brave the Jaws of Doom. RUN ACROSS TWO ROCKS

PUFFIN
puffinbooks.com

ISBN 978-0-141-321332

U.K. £3.99
CAN. $0.00

YOU CAN:
PLAY BOOK BY BOOK
The game is only complete when all seven books in the series are lined up. But if you don't have them all yet, you can still complete the quests! Whoever lands on the 'GO' rock first is the winner of that particular quest.

PLAY THE WHOLE GAME
Whoever collects all seven superpowers and is first to land on the final rock has completed the entire quest and saved Hercules!

REMEMBER:
If you land on a 'Back to the Start' symbol, don't worry – you don't have to go all the way back to book one – just back to the start of the game on the book you are playing.

GOOD LUCK, SUPERHEROES!